A Beautiful Morning

Written by
Johnnie & Michelle Harrison

Illustration by
Vladimir CEBU, LL.B.

Library of Congress Control number: 2020950591

Paperback ISBN: 9781736186107
Hardcover ISBN: 9781736186121

Honey Ink
PUBLISHING, LLC

Dedication

This book is dedicated to Avery, Amir, Peyton and Arlo continue to let your light shine bright!

I wash my hands and my face.
Then I brush my teeth.

I grab my backpack
and I got my lunch too.
I tie my own shoes
now it's time to go to school.

I hop in the car,
then I buckle up.
I hear my favorite song
and I ask my Mom to turn it up!

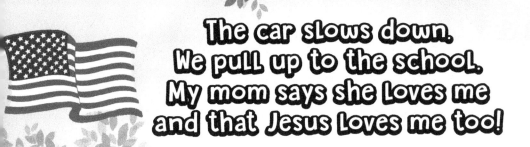

The car slows down.
We pull up to the school.
My mom says she loves me
and that Jesus loves me too!

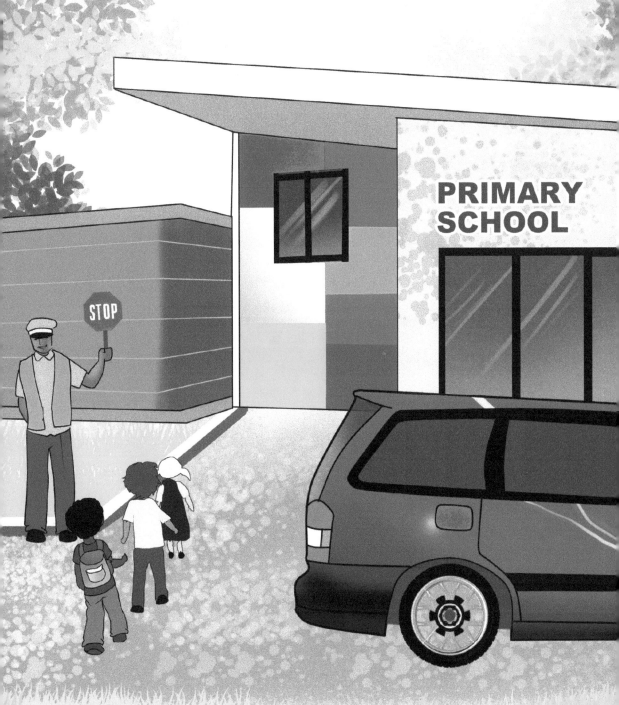

I hop out of the car.
The sun is shining on my face.
I hear the school bell ring
School is going to be great!

Today will be a good day!

CPSIA information can be obtained
at www.ICGtesting.com
Printed in the USA
BVHW021415060521
606649BV00010B/1901